Hello Kitty Pony Surprise!

by Brian James

Illustrated by Sachiho Hino

SCHOLASTIC INC.

New York   Toronto   London   Auckland   Sydney
Mexico City   New Delhi   Hong Kong   Buenos Aires

You can
decorate all of the pictures in this
book with stickers. The page
numbers on the sticker
pages will help you
figure out which
stickers to use.

ISBN 0-439-67632-0

12 11 10 9 8 7 6 5 4 3   40   10 11 12 13 14 15/0

Printed in the U.S.A.
First printing, September 2004

T	W	T	F	S
28	29	30	31	⭐1 Birthday!
4	5	6	7	8
11	12	13	14	15
17	18	19	20	21	22

Hello Kitty was happy.

Her birthday was one week away!

Mama asked Hello Kitty and Mimmy
what they wanted.

"I want a pony!" Hello Kitty said.

"I want a party!" Mimmy said.

Hello Kitty and Mimmy are twins.

They have the same birthday.

Hello Kitty loved ponies.

Mimmy loved parties.

They hoped Mama would say yes.

"Please!" said Hello Kitty and Mimmy.

"We'll see," said Mama.

Hello Kitty wished for a pony all week long.
She wore her cowgirl hat.

She wore her cowgirl boots and vest.

Hello Kitty liked being a cowgirl.

Hello Kitty's friends all said she looked cool.

"My birthday is this Saturday,"
Hello Kitty said. "I asked Mama for a pony!"

At recess, Fifi asked if she could ride the pony.

"I want to ride it, too," Tippy said.

"Everyone can ride my pony,"
Hello Kitty said.

"Yay!" they shouted.

On Friday night, Hello Kitty looked for clues.

She peeked in the backyard.

She peeked in her closet.

She did not find a pony.

Hello Kitty and Mimmy woke up on
Saturday.

"Happy birthday!" Mama said.

Papa said they should wear
their cowgirl outfits.

"We're going out," Mama said.

"Where are we going?" Hello Kitty asked.

"It's a surprise," Papa said.

Hello Kitty and Mimmy loved surprises.

Papa drove to a farm.

It was a pony farm.

Fifi and Tippy were there.

"SURPRISE!" they shouted.

The farmer said everyone would get
a pony ride.

He told them each to pick a pony.

Hello Kitty picked her favorite one.

"Saddle up!" the farmer said.

Hello Kitty climbed on her pony.

Fifi, Tippy, and Mimmy climbed on their ponies, too.

The ponies took them around the farm.

Next they went through the woods.

Then they went back to the barn.

Mama was waiting for Hello Kitty and
Mimmy.

"I know you really wanted a pony," Mama
said to Hello Kitty.

"I know you really wanted a party,"
Mama said to Mimmy.

"This is perfect," Hello Kitty said, "because
Mimmy and I shared our gifts!"

Mama and Papa were very happy.

Hello Kitty and Mimmy were very happy, too.

"I love you, Mama and Papa," said
Hello Kitty.

"I love you, too," said Mimmy.

"We love you both," said Mama and Papa.
"Happy birthday!"